MR. MISCHIEF
and the Leprechaun

Roger Hargreaves

Original concept by
Roger Hargreaves

Written and illustrated by
Adam Hargreaves

EGMONT

Mr Mischief got up bright and early yesterday morning and went into his bathroom for his morning shower.

However, a strange thing happened.

When he turned on the hot water tap, the water came out cold and when he turned on the cold water tap, it came out hot.

Mr Mischief was very puzzled.

When he went downstairs there was another surprise waiting for him in the kitchen.

The surprise was a little old man, all dressed in green, sitting at his kitchen table eating his toast and drinking his tea.

"Who are you?" asked Mr Mischief. "And what are you doing in my house?"

"I'm a Leprechaun, and I've come to stay. Did you enjoy your shower?" chuckled the uninvited guest.

"No! I did not!" exclaimed Mr Mischief, and then the penny dropped. "It was you who swapped my taps round!"

The Leprechaun grinned in answer.

Mr Mischief poured himself a bowl of cornflakes,
sprinkled some sugar on top and began to eat.

"Ugh!" he cried, pulling a disgusted face.
"You've swapped the sugar for the salt!"

The Leprechaun grinned again.

And then Mr Mischief grinned.

"I have to take my hat off to you," said Mr Mischief,
admiringly. "You've got the better of me and I thought
I was the king of mischief."

Suddenly, a thought occurred to Mr Mischief.

"What are you doing today?" he asked.

"Not a lot," replied the Leprechaun.

"How would you like to join me in a bit of mischief making?"

"Now you're talking," said the Leprechaun.

Mr Mischief and the Leprechaun had a wonderful day together.

A wonderful day of mischief.

They offered to take Mr Muddle's photograph.

"Step forwards a bit," said Mr Mischief.

"Forwards a bit more," added the Leprechaun.

And Mr Muddle, being Mr Muddle, stepped backwards a bit and then backwards a bit more and then…

SPLASH!

Poor Mr Muddle.

They poured custard into Little Miss Tiny's home.

WHOOSH!

Poor Little Miss Tiny!

They asked Mr Strong to open a tin of paint for them, but they had already loosened the lid.

SPLAT!

Poor Mr Strong.

They gave Mr Sneeze a sandwich.

A pepper sandwich!

ATISHOO!

Poor Mr Sneeze.

And they meddled with the traffic lights, so they turned green at the same time.

CRASH!

Poor Mr Uppity's car was squashed by Mr Slow's steamroller.

"I've had such a good time," said the Leprechaun at the end of the day, "that I would like to share something with you. As you might know, we Leprechauns keep our gold buried at the end of the rainbow. Will you help me dig it up?"

At that moment a rainbow appeared in the sky and one end fell at their feet.

Mr Mischief agreed immediately and began to dig a hole at the end of the rainbow.

He dug.

And he dug.

And he dug.

And all the while, the Leprechaun sat watching at the edge of the ever deepening hole.

Once Mr Mischief had dug a very deep hole, he looked up at the Leprechaun and asked, "Where's this pot of gold, then?"

"Oh, the gold? Why that's at the other end of the rainbow, don't you know?" laughed the Leprechaun, and he disappeared in a puff of green smoke.

Mr Mischief was left at the bottom of the very deep hole to contemplate the lesson he had learned.

And I hope that you have learnt the same lesson.

A very useful lesson.

Never trust a Leprechaun!